The Great Cat Chase

Written and illustrated by Mercer Mayer

GINGHAM DOG PRESS

Columbus, Ohio

Children's Publishing

Text © 1994 Mercer Mayer
Illustrations © 1974 Mercer Mayer
Cover Illustrations © 1974 Mercer Mayer

This edition published in the United States of America in 2003 by
Gingham Dog Press
an imprint of McGraw-Hill Children's Publishing,
a Division of The McGraw-Hill Companies
8787 Orion Place
Columbus, Ohio 43240-4027

www.MHkids.com

Library of Congress Cataloging-in-Publication Data on file with the publisher.

 A Big Tuna Trading Company, LLC/J.R. Sansevere Book

Printed in The United States of America.

1-57768-358-7

1 2 3 4 5 6 7 8 9 10 PHXBK 08 07 06 05 04 03 02

The McGraw-Hill Companies

IN MEMORY OF MUSO
WHO WAS EVERYTHING A CAT SHOULD BE

One day Sarah Jane took Kitty for a ride . . .
but Kitty was not happy.

So Kitty ran away . . .

and hid from Sarah Jane.

"Help! Help!" said Sarah Jane.

"Kitty ran away."

"There's Kitty," said the policeman.

"Here Kitty, Kitty," he said.

But Kitty did not listen.

Kitty ran away. . . .

And everyone followed . . .

Kitty.

"Whoa! Where did Kitty go?"
asked the policeman.

"That way," said Sarah Jane.

"Help me!" said Sarah Jane.

"I'm falling."

Splash went Sarah Jane and the policeman,
just as Kitty came back.

"There goes Kitty!" said Sarah Jane.

Sarah Jane crawled back into the pipe.

And just as she thought,
Kitty was on the other side.

Kitty jumped on the policeman . . .

and then climbed up a tree.

"Oh no!" said Sarah Jane. "Kitty will fall."

"Gotcha!" said the policeman . . .

as he started to . . .

fall.

"Come with me," said Sarah Jane.

"I know just what we need."

"Milk and cookies for everyone!"